The Forgotten 5

Delano's Prey

M.Y. Hauger

Introduction

It wasn't so long ago when Damien had turned up missing. Kurtis, who was his father, was devastated by his son's disappearance. He suspected that his brother, Endymion, was the one who was responsible for his son's disappearance. Kurtis wanted to find Damien and bring him home, so he decided to form a search party.

Not long after Kurtis had left, Endymion showed up and took over the community. Conner hated what had happened, so he took his nephew Cullen, and left to search for Kurtis.

Endymion didn't stay in the area for very long. He left to take over the other parts of the world, and then, he set out to search for those who had gone missing. Unfortunately, he found Cullen, who was his nephew, dead. With a heavy heart, Endymion took his nephew and laid him to rest.

When Kurtis had returned, he discovered that Endymion had arrested several members of the community, including Steven, who was the leader of the community. Endymion's sons, Aston and Afansi, found those whom their father had arrested and put into his dungeon. The two of them set them free and took them to an underground shelter that they had built in order to keep hidden.

When they returned, Kurtis noticed that Aston was carrying Steven, who was put into a deep sleep. Kurtis took him, put him on a bed and tried to wake him, but it was no use. Steven remained asleep.

Eventually, Steven came out of his deep sleep, but he was not alright, for he was hallucinating that his brother, who was Kurtis' father, was there. At that moment, Steven Jr. told Kurtis that he had to step up and assume the role as the leader of the community. Kurtis didn't want to do it, even though Steven Jr. pointed out that it was agreed upon that if something would happen to Steven, Kurtis would become the leader. With a heavy heart, he reluctantly stepped up and assumed the role of leader of the community.

Chapter 1

Endymion continued to search for those who went missing. One of his brother's sons went with him to help him. They ended up finding a young man named Liam, who was near death. Endymion took him to where he could be healed, and then he took him to his home, where he took care of him. He put Liam into his dungeon because he knew that he was his rival, Levi's son.

When Liam found out the truth about his father, and the things that he had done, he had great remorse. Endymion had compassion on the young man, and he decided to show him mercy, regardless of who he was. He released Liam from his dungeon and treated him as a guest instead of a prisoner. As time went on, the two of them developed a father-son bond, and Liam remained loyal to him.

Liam told Endymion about an evil man named Del, who actually went by the name Delano. He told Endymion that Del had bitten him, and that he had fangs and venom glands. Liam also told him about the dark, ominous vibe that Del gave whenever he was nearby. Endymion had stated that he felt a similar vibe whenever he spotted his dead nephew, whom he had laid to rest.

Endymion wanted to know more about Del. He wanted to know where he came from, but Liam didn't know. Endymion suspected that Del was the one who was responsible for all the trouble, and he wanted to find him, and stop him before he ended up hurting anyone else.

Chapter 2

It was true that Delano had killed Cullen. He had also taken Damien, Zane, and Conner as his prisoners and he had been keeping them in his dungeon. He wanted to make them miserable because he was miserable. Delano had lost his wife and children, all on the same day. His wife had been shot with an arrow when she rushed over to Delano and got in front of him to prevent him from being shot. Then, his children were chased by the same men who killed his wife. Delano never saw his children again. He searched for them, but he never found them. Because of what had happened, Delano had become bitter and full of wrath. He wanted to cause others pain because of the pain that he had felt.

Then, he started having strange dreams and other peculiar things started to happen. Delano wanted answers, so he left his home. He overheard people talking about a future warrior. Delano wasn't sure why, but just hearing about this individual caused him to feel threatened. He left the area, and he went to the dungeon to confront his prisoners about it. They told him that they knew nothing about it.

That evening, Conner overheard Damien talking to Zane about the future warrior. When Damien and Zane had fallen asleep, Delano showed up in the dungeon, and he took Conner to his room, where they talked. Conner told him that he overheard Damien talking about the future warrior. He also told him that he didn't exist yet, but he was supposed to come into the world several generations later. Conner also told Delano that the future warrior was to be born through Endymion's bloodline. Conner went on to tell him about a set of Endymion's twins who lived in the community where he had come from. He told him their names, which were Aston and Afansi. Conner told him that they wouldn't be hard to spot due to their unique appearance. At that moment, Delano had his mind set on finding Aston and Afansi. He wanted to make sure the future warrior would never have a chance to exist.

Chapter 3

Kurtis decided to continue his search for Damien, Cullen, and Conner. Aston, Afansi, Steve, and Edgar went with him. Kurtis decided to leave Steven Jr. in charge while he was away. Steven Jr. volunteered his twin brother, Simon, to help him watch over everyone and everything.

Endymion was not in the area during that time because he and Liam had decided to continue their search for those who had gone missing. They also wanted to find Delano, so they could put an end to the destruction that he was causing. At first, Endymion didn't want

Liam to go with him because he knew that it would be dangerous for him. He knew that Delano bit Liam with the intent to kill him. Endymion also realized that if Delano knew that Liam was still alive, he would surely try to kill him again. Liam refused to take no for an answer, and he told Endymion that he was willing to give his life for him. Knowing that there was no talking him out of it, Endymion agreed to let him come with him.

Meanwhile, Delano decided to go back to the neighborhood to see if he could spot Endymion's sons. He made sure to keep himself hidden because he didn't want to be discovered. Delano snuck around as he checked every house, but he saw no sign of either of them. He became frustrated with his lack of success. Delano was about to leave when he glanced toward the huge house where he had been before. At first, he was reluctant to go there, but then he decided to go inside. He teleported into the house, and he snuck around as he searched for Endymion's sons, but he didn't find them. Then he spotted the woman who had caught his attention the last time he was there. He remained hidden as he watched her for a moment. Then he disappeared before he would be spotted, and he decided to go back to his home.

Chapter 4

When Delano returned, he started to pace the floor. He became more and more frustrated as he thought about how he had not spotted Endymion's sons. Then he stopped what he was doing for a moment as he thought, and then he teleported to the dungeon. Right away, he looked at Conner before he pointed at him.

"You! Come." Delano said.

Without hesitation, Conner stood up and made his way over to him. With an angry expression on his face, Delano took hold of him before they both vanished.

"Sit down." Delano said.

Conner sat down as he kept his eyes on Delano.

"We need to talk." Delano said.

"I know that you're frustrated, but you need to be patient."

"I'm not a patient man!" Delano said.

He sighed, and then he put his hand on his forehead for a moment. Then he looked at Conner as he spoke.

"I don't know what it is that I'm supposed to be looking for. You said that I wouldn't miss them, yet I saw nothing out of the ordinary." Delano said.

"But they're not ordinary. They look like him."

"I'm unique! If I wasn't a master at keeping hidden, I'd stick out like a sore thumb! As for everyone in that community, they just look like ordinary people."

"I'm telling you that you would know them if you saw them."

"How so?" Delano asked.

"They have purple skin like their father."

"Purple skin?"

"Yes. Theirs is a bit lighter than his, and their hair color is a bit lighter than his."

"Is that so?"

"Yes, but I must tell you that Endymion can copy himself. If you see anyone who looks exactly like him, they are not his sons. They're his copies."

"Are they able to have children?" Delano asked.

"I don't know, but it doesn't matter because this person whom you're worried about is to be born through Afansi's or Aston's bloodline."

"Do either of them have children?" Delano asked.

"Not that I know of." Conner said.

"Then I know what I must do. I must keep an eye out for them. When I spot them, I will put a stop to this thing once and for all."

Chapter 5

Several days had passed and Kurtis and his search party had returned. Everyone could see the disappointment in Kurtis' face as he walked toward his home. He tried to remain strong as he fought back tears. He missed his sons, and he hated that they were still missing. Kurtis wanted to find them, so they could be brought home, but there was no sign of them anywhere. He sighed as he opened the door and went inside, followed by Aston and Afansi. When Veda saw the look on her husband's face, she made her way over to him and gave him a hug.

"I didn't find them. It's like they've fallen off the face of this earth." Kurtis said.

He then broke down and wept. Aston and Afansi glanced at one another with sorrowful expressions on their faces, then they both looked at Kurtis. Tears filled Veda's eyes as she hugged her husband tightly. None of them wanted to accept the possibility that they would never see Damien and the others again. Just then, Rose, who was Aston's wife, and Ivy, who was Afansi's wife, came into the room. They both made their way over to their husbands and hugged them. Aston hugged Rose tightly, and then he gave her a kiss.

"I missed you so much." Rose said.

"I missed you too." Aston said.

Ivy looked Afansi in the eyes, and then she smiled.

"I know that it's bad timing, but I have something that I need to tell you." Ivy said.

"What is it?" Afansi asked.

"I'd rather talk to you about it alone."

"Oh." Afansi said.

He then glanced at his twin brother, who looked over at him as he hugged Rose. Afansi glanced at his wife before he looked at Kurtis.

"Do you mind if Ivy and I step outside?" Afansi asked.

"No, just be careful." Kurtis said.

He then glanced at Ivy. Even though he had tears running down his face, he managed to smile at her before he looked at Afansi, still with a smile on his face.

"Will you be alright?" Afansi asked.

"I'll be fine, son. You go and have your talk. You have my blessing." Kurtis said.

Afansi was bewildered by Kurtis' comment. He took hold of Ivy's hand before the two of them went outside.

"Would you like to go to our quiet place to talk?" Afansi asked.

"Yes." Ivy said.

The two of them continued to walk as they headed toward the quiet spot. When they got there, Ivy took hold of both of Afansi's hands as she looked into his eyes.

"I missed you so much." Afansi said.

"I missed you too."

"What did you need to talk about?"

"How do you feel about being a father?"

"I don't know. I've never really thought about it." Afansi said.

Suddenly, he had a surprised expression on his face.

"Wait! Are you trying to tell me that I'm going to be a father?" Afansi said.

"Yes." Ivy said.

Afansi had a big smile on his face as he hugged his wife.

"I can't believe it! I'm going to be a father! This is the happiest day of my life!" Afansi said.

He then gave her a kiss.

"Is that why Kurtis told me that we have his blessing?" Afansi asked.

"I never told Kurtis."

"Oh."

"You're the only one that I told. I felt that you should be the first one to know."

"I can't wait to tell everyone! Of course, I think I'm going to wait a bit. I don't feel like it's the appropriate time. Kurtis is really upset about not finding Damien and the others. Actually, I'm sad about it, too. What if they're never found? Damien is like a brother to me, and he won't even be a part of our children's lives."

"I'm so sorry."

"It's not your fault. It's great news about becoming a father, but it's sad that Damien isn't here. I miss him so much."

"Everybody does."

"I wish there was a way to know where he's at, but it's like Kurtis said. It's as if he and the others had fallen off the face of the earth. For all we know, they could be dead."

"But we don't know that." Ivy said.

"Yes, I know, and I'd like to believe that they're still alive, but at the moment, I'm not so sure anymore." Afansi said.

Ivy touched the side of Afansi's face before she gave him a hug.

"Can we stay out here for a while? I think I'd just like to spend some time here alone with you." Afansi said.

"Yes." Ivy said.

She took hold of his hand and the two of them walked over to the huge tree where they both sat down together for several hours.

Chapter 6

Meanwhile, Kurtis decided to go to Steven's house to see how he was doing. When he got there, he knocked on the door, and then Steven Jr. answered it shortly afterward.

"Hello, Junior." Kurtis said.

"Hey, Kurtis."

"How's he doing?" Kurtis asked.

With a sorrowful expression on his face, Steven Jr. just shook his head.

"Could this get any worse? We may never find my sons or Conner. It's like a never-ending nightmare."

"I know, Kurtis. I wish there would be something that could make things better." Steven Jr. said.

Kurtis said nothing as he looked at him.

"On the bright side, I haven't seen Endymion around." Steven Jr. said.

"I'm not so sure if that is a bright side, seeing as he was probably the one who took them in the first place. He'd be the only one who knows where they are." Kurtis said.

"Are you going to be alright?"

"I have to try to remain strong. Sometimes, it's just so hard."

"I understand. Take care of yourself."

"I'll try." Kurtis said.

He then left Steven's house and headed back to his own home.

Chapter 7

Several hours had passed, and Afansi and Ivy returned to Kurtis' home. Afansi opened the door and then he and Ivy went inside. They walked into the kitchen together, hand in hand.

"You're just in time for dinner. For a moment, I wasn't sure whether you would be back in time. I thought I would have to go out after you." Kurtis said.

"We were just at the quiet place." Afansi said.

"I figured that." Kurtis said.

He then started to serve soup that he had prepared. Afterward, they gave thanks before they ate.

"It's as delicious as ever." Afansi said.

"Thank you." Kurtis said.

Everything was quiet for a moment until Afansi broke the silence.

"I have something that I want to tell you." he said.

He could see that Kurtis was trying to hold back a smile.

"If it's a bad time, I can wait." Afansi said.

"No, son. Go ahead." Kurtis said.

"Earlier today, Ivy told me that she had something that she needed to tell me. That's the reason we stepped outside."

"I figured that."

"At first, I wasn't sure what to expect. When we got to our quiet spot, she gave me some good news." Afansi said.

Kurtis said nothing as he smiled.

"I'm going to be a father." Afansi said.

"Is it true?" Aston asked.

"I know that it seems like a dream, but it is true." Afansi said.

"Congratulations. I'm happy for you." Aston said.

He smiled at his twin brother. Kurtis glanced at Aston with an expression of concern on his face. Even though Aston was smiling, he could see the pain in his eyes.

"Are you alright, Aston?" Kurtis asked.

"I'm fine. As I said, I'm happy for Afansi." Aston said.

Then Kurtis glanced at Afansi and smiled.

"We're all happy for you, son, and as I said earlier, you have my blessing." Kurtis said.

"Thank you. You have no idea how happy this makes me. This is the happiest day of my life."

Chapter 8

The next day, Aston and Afansi both took their wives to their secret place, where they met Steve with his wife, Jasmine.

"It seems like it's been a while since we've been here." Steve said.

"Afansi was here just yesterday." Aston said.

"Why didn't you invite the rest of us? It would've been good for all of us." Steve said.

"Ivy and I needed some time alone, which brings me to the next thing." Afansi said.

"Which is…" Steve said.

"I'm going to be a father." Afansi said.

"What?" Steve said.

"It's true. Ivy told me the news yesterday. Isn't it great?" Afansi said.

"Yes, it is great news. Congratulations." Steve said.

"Perhaps we could celebrate." Afansi said.

"Do you think it would be appropriate to celebrate?" Aston asked.

"Why not?" Afansi asked.

"Steve's grandfather isn't well, and there are still people missing." Aston said.

"I realize that, but I thought it would be nice to do something positive in light of all the negativity that we've been dealing with." Afansi said.

Aston didn't respond.

"Aren't you happy for me?" Afansi asked.

"Of course I am. I told you that I was yesterday, it's just that it isn't fair to Steve's grandfather, and it's just not the same without Damien." Aston said.

"I'm sorry. I suppose I wasn't thinking about that because I was happy about the good news." Afansi said.

"I think we should just wait." Aston said.

He then glanced at Steve.

"We should wait for Steve's grandfather to get better, and we should also wait until we find the others." Aston said.

Steve glanced down at the ground with a sorrowful expression on his face.

"I miss Damien." Aston said.

Steve then glanced at Aston, still with an expression of sorrow on his face.

"I know. We all miss him." Steve said.

Aston cupped his hands to his face as he broke down and wept. Rose hugged her husband as he cried.

Chapter 9

The group of young men didn't know that they were being watched. Delano decided to go back out to the quiet spot that he found to be mysterious. There, he spotted Endymion's sons. He kept himself hidden as he watched them closely while they carried on with their conversation. When they left, Delano also left, and he went back to his home. He thought for a moment before he went to the dungeon. Delano approached Conner and then the two of them vanished and Delano took Conner to his room where they would usually talk alone.

"I finally spotted them." Delano said.

"You have?" Conner asked.

"Yes, and what's more, I overheard one of them saying that he was going to be a father."

"What?"

"It's true. I guess I know which one the future warrior is supposed to be born through."

"You do?"

"Yes. It all makes sense. It has to be him. It could never be the other one. He seems weak."

"What makes you say that?" Conner asked.

"He's a crybaby. I saw him break down. And for what? He was crying about Damien, of all things."

"I once heard that Damien and Endymion's sons are very close. They're like brothers. There's also another guy named Steve."

"I did see one other man there. I'm assuming that it was this Steve that you speak of."

"Most likely. Did you see anything else?"

"I saw three beautiful women there. I'm assuming they are the men's wives."

"Probably."

"They weren't as beautiful as the woman that had captured my attention, and none of them are as beautiful as my Lela was, but I would take any of them later on. Now is not the time. It is still too soon."

"So, you think you know which of the brothers the warrior will be born through." Conner said.

"I know which one it certainly isn't. I don't need to worry about him. My focus will be on the one who's to become a father. I will make sure his descendants never have the chance to exist."

Chapter 10

As time went on, Kurtis became more and more concerned about Aston. Even though Aston tried to hide it, Kurtis could see that something was making him sorrowful. He could also sense his pain, and it was intense. Aston kept quiet about what was hurting him. He was genuinely happy about his brother's good news, but whenever he smiled, his eyes remained sad. Kurtis could see the pain that was deep in Aston's eyes. He wanted to help him, but he wasn't sure how. Kurtis often asked him if he was alright, and he would tell him that he was fine, but Kurtis knew better.

One day, Kurtis decided to ask him again.

"Aston, are you alright?" Kurtis asked.

"I'm fine." Aston said.

"Are you sure? The reason I ask is that I can't help but notice that you seem depressed."

"I'll be alright."

"Are you sure?" Kurtis asked.

"Yes. I think I'm going to head outside for some fresh air." Aston said.

He then walked away and went outside.

Chapter 11

Later that day, Kurtis decided to go to his quiet place because he had a lot on his mind and he just wanted some time alone. He walked toward it, but then he stopped for a moment. As he stood there, he thought for a moment before he decided to go through the tunnel. He continued to walk until he had gotten to the end where one would have to climb out. There, he spotted Aston sitting with his head down on his knees.

"Aston?" Kurtis said.

Aston looked at Kurtis with tears running down his face.

"Aston? What's the matter?" Kurtis asked.

His expression was sorrowful, and his heart sank as he looked into Aston's sad eyes.

"I'd rather not talk about it." Aston said.

"Please, son. I know that you're hurting. Talk to me."

"I can't." Aston said.

Kurtis fought back tears as he kept his eyes on the young man.

"Very well. I understand if you don't want to talk about it. I just want you to know that you're not alone in your pain." Kurtis said.

He was about to walk away when Aston spoke.

"Rose and I can't have children." Aston said.

Kurtis stopped, and then he turned and looked at Aston.

"It can't be." Kurtis said.

"Unfortunately, it's true." Aston said.

"Are you sure?"

"We've tried numerous times, but we can't."

"Perhaps the timing is wrong."

"No, Kurtis. It's because of me. I know that for a fact."

"You don't know that."

"I do. There's something wrong with me and because of it, I'll never become a father." Aston said.

Kurtis fought back tears as he looked at him.

"It can't be. It has to be a mistake." Kurtis said.

"I truly wish that it was, but unfortunately, it's not."

"I'm so sorry, son." Kurtis said.

Aston cupped his hands to his face as he wept.

What the two of them didn't notice was that there were three other people who were close by, and they were hidden. One of them was pleased about what he was hearing. The other two were devastated and heartbroken about what they had heard. Their hearts sank, and their eyes welled up with tears as they listened to the conversation.

"Where have I gone wrong? What have I done to deserve this?" Aston asked.

"You've done nothing wrong, son."

"I feel like I'm being judged."

"Why?"

"Because I upset my father. I probably hurt him whenever I left him." Aston said.

At that moment, one of the individuals who was hidden cupped his hands to his face as he broke down and wept. The one who was pleased with the bad news smirked as he watched what was happening.

"You've done nothing wrong, son. You're an adult, and it was your choice to move out and start your own life."

"But he never wanted us to leave."

"But that's not his choice. He can't make all your decisions for you." Kurtis said.

Tears ran down Aston's face as he looked at Kurtis.

"Listen to me. This is not your fault. I don't know why this has happened to you. Sometimes things happen that we don't understand. Oftentimes, we don't have the answers, but I can tell you that it's nothing that you have done." Kurtis said.

"I'll never experience the joys of being a father."

"I'm very sorry, son. I wish that there was something that I could do for you, but unfortunately, there isn't." Kurtis said.

Aston broke down again, and Kurtis hugged the young man tightly as he wept. Tears filled Kurtis' eyes, and then they streamed down his face as his heart sank deeper. Then, he was suddenly taken back to when Endymion was very young and how he had often spoken of how he wanted a big family.

Kurtis could remember how painful it was to hear him talk about it, knowing at that time, his chances of having what he wanted were slim. At that moment, Kurtis hugged Aston even tighter as his heart sank even deeper as he was reminded of the brother that he missed.

"Kurtis?" Aston said.

"Yes, son?"

"Can you do something for me?"

"What is it, son?"

"Please, don't tell my brother. I don't want him to know." Aston said.

"I won't tell him." Kurtis said.

Meanwhile, the three who were hidden remained quiet. Two of them were full of sorrow, while the other was content with what he had heard. He knew without a doubt which person he had to focus on so that he could accomplish his mission once and for all.

Chapter 12

Later that day, Afansi took Steve aside because he wanted to talk to him.

"Take a walk with me." Afansi said.

"What about Aston?" Steve asked.

"No. I need to talk to you."

"Okay." Steve said.

The two of them started to walk, and Afansi kept glancing back as they walked further away.

"Is there a problem?" Steve asked.

"Yes, but I want to wait until we get further away to talk about it."

"Alright." Steve said.

The two of them continued to walk until Afansi felt they had gotten far enough away, and then they stopped.

"So, what's going on?" Steve asked.

"It's Aston. I overheard some bad news about him."

"I don't like how that sounds."

"I overheard him telling Kurtis that he and Rose are unable to have children."

"What?"

"It came as a shock to me too. He told Kurtis that there's something wrong with him, and he's the reason they couldn't have children."

"That's terrible." Steve said.

"I know. I can't get over how sad he was. It was heartbreaking."

"I feel sad for him."

"I know. What I don't understand is why he doesn't want to tell me about it? He asked Kurtis not to tell me about it. Why would he do that?" Afansi said.

"Could it have to do with the fact that you're able to do what he can't? You're able to have a family while he cannot. He's probably crushed, not to mention the fact that there's a possibility that he may feel like he's inadequate and inferior to you."

"He shouldn't feel that way."

"It could be the reason he's become so melancholic. Haven't you noticed it?"

"Yes, but I figured that it was because he misses Damien."

"I'm sure he does miss Damien. Who doesn't? The thing is, Aston is probably devastated by the fact that he'll never be able to have a family."

"Perhaps I could help him out."

"What do you suggest?" Steve asked.

Afansi just looked at him.

"I don't think that's such a good idea." Steve said.

"I want to help him."

"But it wouldn't be the same for him. They would be yours, and that would probably be in the back of his mind constantly. I'd imagine that he would want them to be his own, otherwise, it would probably make him feel worse. It would be a constant reminder of the fact that he's unable to do what you can. It could even cause him to become angry and resentful if you'd even make such a suggestion. Just think about it. I know that if it was me, I wouldn't be happy about it." Steve said.

"I'm only wanting to help."

"I realize that, but I'd caution you about that."

"Right. It's just that I feel so bad for him. He's so depressed. I haven't seen him so depressed since the time when he had been ambushed by Rose's father."

"That wasn't so long ago."

"It's been so rough for him. To make things worse, he fears that he's being judged."

"What do you mean?" Steve asked.

"He thinks he's being punished for leaving father."

"What?"

"It's true. I heard him telling Kurtis that he fears that he's being judged because of that."

"But that doesn't make sense. If that was the case, then you shouldn't be able to have children either."

"I know. I wouldn't be surprised if father somehow caused Aston to think that."

"Why would he do that?"

"To make him feel guilty."

"I don't know about that. If that was the case, wouldn't he do the same to you?"

"No, and I'll tell you why. Aston's always been the more sensitive one and because of it, father always babied him, I mean, if Aston did so much as sniffle, father was there."

"Did he favor him?"

"No, it wasn't like that at all. It's kind of hard to explain. He babied both of us when we were little, in fact, he wouldn't let us out of his sight. When we got older, he did treat us differently, but it wasn't in a way that would make us feel like he preferred one over the other."

"Oh." Steve said.

Afansi sighed, and then he shook his head before he spoke.

"I feel so sad for Aston. He's done nothing to deserve this. I wish there was something that could be done to make things better for him. He deserves so much better than this."

Chapter 13

After their conversation, Afansi headed back home while Steve headed to the quiet spot. There, he saw Kurtis, who seemed depressed as he sat beneath the huge tree. At first, Steve was hesitant to stay, but then he decided to stay. When he approached Kurtis, he sat down beside him.

"Kurtis?" Steve said.

Kurtis glanced at Steve with a sorrowful expression on his face.

"I heard about Aston. I'm very sorry. I don't even have words to describe the sorrow that I feel for him." Steve said.

"You heard about it?"

"Yes, Afansi told me."

"Afansi told you?"

"Yes. Apparently, he overheard you and Aston talking about it."

"I don't even know what to say. I wish that there was something I could do for him."

"I know."

"You have no idea how depressing this is, and for so many reasons."

"It would be sad for anyone who cares, Aston and Rose most of all."

"He's crushed because of it, and he blames himself."

"I've heard."

"How much did Afansi hear?" Kurtis said.

"Something tells me that he heard pretty much everything."

"I'm so worried about Aston. He becomes so depressed. I'm sure you remember how bad it was after he was ambushed by Rose's father. He wouldn't even eat."

"I know. It is a bit concerning."

"There has to be an intervention. We can't let things get that bad again."

"Perhaps we should have a discussion."

"Right, but I think that we should be careful of who is involved in the discussion."

"I agree."

"I think we should go to Simon's house."

"I agree."

"Also, I want your father to be involved in this discussion because this is a very important matter for various reasons."

"Right." Steve said.

The two of them got up, and then they left the quiet spot to gather the people who they wanted to be a part of the very important discussion.

Chapter 14

After gathering the people who they wanted to be in the discussion, Steve and Kurtis went to Simon's house. When they got there, Kurtis knocked on the door. Simon opened the door, and he seemed perplexed as he glanced at everyone.

"Is there something wrong?" he asked.

"Yes, and we need to have a discussion about it." Kurtis said.

"Okay."

"No, you don't understand. We've decided to have the discussion here." Kurtis said.

"Oh, okay, in that case, come on in." Simon said.

Everyone followed Kurtis into Simon's house. They made their way to the dining room and sat down.

"We didn't interrupt anything, did we?" Kurtis asked.

"No, not at all." Simon said.

Everyone who was there sat down at the table.

"Where's Aston and Afansi? Aren't they usually involved?" Simon asked.

"Yeah, that's true. Where are they?" Hank asked.

"Actually, the discussion is about them, particularly Aston." Kurtis said.

"Is there something wrong?" Edgar asked.

"Actually, yes, and it's rather serious." Kurtis said.

"What is it, Kurtis?" Simon asked.

At that moment, Kurtis broke down in tears. With an expression of concern on his face, Hank glanced at Edgar.

"What's wrong, Kurtis? Obviously, something has made you upset." Edgar said.

"We've heard some bad news about Aston." Steve said.

"What is it, son?" Steven Jr. asked.

"He and Rose are unable to have children." Steve said.

Steven Jr.'s heart sank.

"Are you sure about this?" he asked.

"Afansi told me about it." Steve said.

Steven Jr. then glanced at Kurtis.

"It's true. Aston himself told me so." Kurtis said.

"This is terrible. Wasn't the future warrior supposed to be born through his bloodline?" Hank said.

"Yes." Kurtis said.

"This can't be. It has to be a mistake." Steven Jr. said.

"Not according to what Aston told me. To make things worse, he blames himself. He thinks that he's being judged for leaving his father." Kurtis said.

"What?" Edgar said.

Suddenly, they heard the sound of Levi's voice.

"Endymion probably put that idea in his head." he said.

Hank glanced over, and then he shook his head before he put his hand on his forehead.

"Oh no." he said.

"Levi, what are you doing here?" Kurtis asked.

"I snuck inside because I knew something was going on. By the way, I think you should know that Afansi's looking for you."

"What about Aston?" Kurtis said.

"I don't know. I didn't see him."

"We better make this quick." Kurtis said.

"Is there anything else we should know?" Hank asked.

"I'm very concerned about Aston. I fear that he will fall into depression. The last time that happened, he wouldn't eat." Kurtis said.

"This is not good." Hank said.

"But what should we do?" We can't force him to eat." Edgar said.

"We have to be supportive of him. I have no doubt that this is going to be a difficult time for him. The conversation with him was heart-wrenching. He was crushed." Kurtis said.

"I'm going to say that it's depressing for all of us. If he and Rose are unable to have children, how is this supposed future leader ever supposed to exist?" Levi said.

"He won't. Not, unless Junior made a mistake." Kurtis said.

"How so?" Hank asked.

"Afansi is expecting to become a father. Perhaps he could come from his bloodline instead." Kurtis said.

"Well, that's some good news, right?" Hank said.

"Yes, but it wasn't a mistake. The future warrior was to be born through Aston's line." Steven Jr. said.

"Well, obviously that can't be right if Aston and Rose can't even have children." Hank said.

"Yes, and although I'm very happy for Afansi, I'm extremely sad for Aston. It's great that Afansi will have a family, but that's something that Aston also wants, something that he will never have." Kurtis said.

"This is terrible. It probably makes the blow even worse for poor Aston." Edgar said.

"Yes, and it's probably the reason that Aston didn't want Afansi to know about it." Kurtis said.

"I tried to explain that to Afansi." Steve said.

Hank then glanced at something from the corner of his eye.

"Don't look now, but I thought you should know that we have company." he said.

Kurtis glanced at the entrance of the room and saw both Aston and Afansi standing there.

"What's going on?" Aston asked.

Kurtis said nothing as he looked at Aston with a sorrowful expression on his face.

"Does Afansi know about Rose and I not being able to have children?" Aston asked.

Nobody responded.

"Did you tell him about it?" Aston asked.

"No, he didn't." Afansi said.

Then Aston turned and glanced at his brother.

"Afansi?" Aston said.

"Kurtis didn't tell me about it." Afansi said.

"Then who told you about it?"

"Nobody did. I overheard you and Kurtis talking about it." Afansi said.

"Were you eavesdropping?"

"Yes."

"Why?"

"I knew that there was something wrong. I was worried about you, so I followed you. I kept myself hidden, so you wouldn't see me." Afansi said.

Aston fought back tears as he looked at his brother.

"Why wouldn't you tell me?" Afansi asked.

"I tried to explain that to you, Afansi." Steve said.

Afansi became teary-eyed as he looked at his twin brother.

"Whatever it is that you're thinking, it isn't true." Afansi said.

At that moment, Aston broke down and wept, and Afansi hugged him.

"I'm here for you." Afansi said.

Kurtis then got up and walked over to them and hugged them.

"I'm here for you too." Kurtis said.

"We're all here for you." Edgar said.

"It's true. Don't ever think that you'll have to go through this alone." Simon said.

"I miss Damien. I wish he was here." Aston said.

Tears ran down Kurtis' face as he spoke.

"I know, son. We all do. I realize that the two of you became close. He would've wanted to be here for you. I know he would've. I'm not about to give up. I will keep searching for him."

Chapter 15

Kurtis decided to search for his sons and Conner again. He took the same people with him that he had taken the last time. Once again, Steven Jr. and Simon were left in charge of things while Kurtis and his search party were away.

Kurtis and his search party spent several days looking for those who were missing, but they found no sign of them. When they returned, Kurtis could tell right away that something was wrong.

"Junior, what's going on?" Kurtis asked.

"Kurtis, it's awful." Simon said.

"What is it?" Kurtis asked.

"It's Ivy. She's gone." Steven Jr. said.

At that moment, Kurtis' heart sank.

"What?" he said.

"It happened the day after you left. Veda rushed over to Simon's and told him that Ivy was gone. Before she told him about it, she and Rose searched the neighborhood, but there was no sign of her." Steven Jr. said.

"No." Kurtis said.

"We sent several men out to look for her. They haven't returned." Simon said.

Just then, Aston and Afansi approached them.

"What's going on?" Aston asked.

Kurtis' eyes welled up with tears as he looked at the twin brothers.

"It's Ivy. She's missing." Steven Jr. said.

"No, it can't be. Tell me it isn't true." Afansi said.

"I wish we could." Simon said.

At that moment, Afansi took off running to search for his wife. Tears ran down Aston's face as he watched his brother, who frantically searched for his wife. At that moment, he broke down and wept.

"I have to help him." Aston said.

He then left to join his brother in his search for his wife. Tears ran down Kurtis' face as he watched him. He and Steve glanced at one another before they left to help the brothers look for Ivy.

Chapter 16

Delano returned to his home and he was pleased with everything that had happened. He was so happy about it that he decided to go to the dungeon and talk about it.

When Delano appeared in the dungeon, his prisoners noticed the smirk on his face.

"It brings me great pleasure to say that I have won. I will be able to establish my kingdom of darkness." Delano said.

"What do you mean by saying that you won?" Damien asked.

"I mean, there will be no future warrior."

"How do you know?" Damien asked.

Delano said nothing as he looked at him with a grimace on his face.

"What did you do?" Damien asked.

"I made the wife of the one who was going to become a father vanish. His family is no more. As for the other one, he and his wife are unable to have children, so I don't even have to worry about him. I'd kill him, but it's so much better for me to see him suffer. He's miserable and it brings me pleasure. Now, they're both miserable, and I love it." Delano said.

"No." Damien said.

Delano chuckled, and then he vanished before their eyes.

"It can't be true." Damien said.

"How could he be so heartless?" Zane said.

"Look at what he did to us. It's basically the same thing. He tore us from our families. We'll never see our wives again, nor will we ever see our children, and it's all because of him." Damien said.

He then stood up.

"What are you doing?" Zane asked.

"I'm breaking out of here. I must get to Aston and Afansi." Damien said.

"Count me in." Zane said.

Then he stood up.

"Stop!" Conner said.

"Why? So he can ruin more lives?" Damien said.

"You'll never stand a chance." Conner said.

"We can both run quickly." Zane said.

"So? He's faster, seeing as he can teleport." Conner said.

"He must be stopped." Damien said.

"If he catches you, he will surely kill you." Conner said.

"But if we do nothing, we'll never get out. Didn't you hear what he said? He destroyed my brother's family. The future warrior will never exist. All hope is gone." Zane said.

"It just can't be. So many people had talked about him. Now, we're hearing that he'll never exist?" Damien said.

Zane thought for a moment before he spoke.

"Not all hope is lost. There is still one who can save us." Zane said.

"Your father." Damien said.

"Yes. If he ever finds us, he will set us free, and I can promise you that he will put an end to this. He will see to it that Delano's kingdom of darkness will never exist."

Chapter 17

That night, Delano appeared to Conner, who was still awake.

"Come." Delano said.

Conner stood up and walked over to Delano, who then teleported to his room. Then he glanced at Conner as he spoke.

"Sit down." Delano said.

Conner did as he was told.

"I want to thank you for what you've done for me. As much as I hate to admit it, you've made it, so I could be successful in my mission to defeat my enemy." Delano said.

"I wanted to help you."

"I am grateful to you. You've been a loyal servant to me. Because of that, once I have my kingdom of darkness established, I may consider the possibility of allowing you to be free from the dungeon, as long as you promise never to try to escape." Delano said.

"I'll never try to escape, no matter what." Conner said.

"I admire your loyalty."

"I'd do anything for you. I'd even lay down my life for you."

"Is that so?"

"Yes."

"Perhaps, when the time comes for me to find a woman, I could find one for you as well."

"Would you really do that for me?"

"Of course, after all, you've earned it."

"I would like that very much."

"Have you ever been with a woman?"

"No, I haven't."

"Somehow, I'm not surprised."

"I suppose you'll probably want to take me back to the dungeon now."

"On the contrary, I was going to reward you by letting you free for the night, but if you prefer to be in the dungeon, I'll take you back."

"No, I would rather be free."

"You do realize that if I catch you trying to escape, I will kill you."

"I already told you that I'd never try to escape." Conner said.

"We shall see."

Chapter 18

It was a day later when Kurtis, Aston, Afansi, and Steve returned. All of them had sorrowful expressions on their faces as they headed to Simon's house. When they got there, Kurtis knocked on the door. Simon answered it right away.

"Can you and Junior gather everyone? I think it's time for a meeting." Kurtis said.

"Yes." Simon said.

Kurtis and the others then went back to Kurtis' house and waited patiently for Simon and Steven Jr. to show up. It was fifteen minutes later when they showed up.

"Please, come inside." Kurtis said.

Everyone could see that the situation was taking a toll on him.

"As some of you may know, Afansi's wife, Ivy, is missing. Several of us searched for her, but she was nowhere to be found." Kurtis said.

"Isn't it obvious? Endymion took her. He's the one who's responsible for all the disappearances." Levi said.

"But why?" Simon asked.

"Most likely for revenge because Aston and Afansi left him and chose to stay with us." Levi said.

Afansi and Aston both frowned because neither of them wanted to believe that their father would do such a thing."

"It seems like he won't stop. That's why we have to stop him." Levi said.

"How? We don't even know where he's at." Kurtis said.

"Have any of you seen him around?" Steve asked.

"No, but that doesn't mean that he didn't do it. He could've done it during the night." Levi said.

"Maybe he did do it. We all know that he wasn't happy about us leaving." Afansi said.

"That's right." Levi said.

"I don't know. It doesn't seem to make sense to me." Steve said.

"Why? I think it makes a lot of sense. Endymion is a vindictive monster."

"Possibly, but if he was going to seek revenge, wouldn't he just approach them? Furthermore, why would he stop at just Afansi? Why didn't he take Rose? She's Aston's wife." Steve said.

"For one thing, Aston and Afansi weren't here. Second of all, they can teleport, so arresting them would do no good. Third of all, I'd say he was trying to hit where it hurts the most, especially seeing as Afansi was going to be a father." Levi said.

"Still, why wouldn't he take Rose?" Steve asked.

"She's not expecting."

"So? She's still Aston's family, whether she's expecting or not."

"What's your point?"

"I'm just saying that what you're saying makes absolutely no sense. If he was going to hit where it hurts, as you say, wouldn't he have taken Aston's lover as well, seeing as Aston is also his son?" Steve said.

"He's already sought his revenge on him."

"How so?" Steve asked.

"By making it, so Aston can't have a family."

"Do you have proof of that?"

"Well, no, but I wouldn't put it past him to do such a thing." Levi said.

"Somehow, I find it hard to believe that he would do that. Furthermore, if he was going to go to such great lengths to seek his revenge, why wouldn't he just take Rose? She's Aston's wife. She's his family, and he loves her. Also, why would he stop there? Why wouldn't he take Veda as well?"

"Because she's Kurtis' wife, not theirs."

"So? Wouldn't it make sense that if he was going to seek revenge on his sons, he would also seek revenge on the man whom they chose to stay with."

"He already sought his revenge on Kurtis by taking Damien and Cullen." Levi said.

"Did he?" Steve asked.

"Can we stop arguing? This is solving nothing. What we need to do is figure out what to do about this." Kurtis said.

"We could send more men to search for her." Simon said.

"Perhaps, although we haven't had much luck so far." Kurtis said.

"The problem is, without knowing where he is or where he's putting the people that he's taking, I'm not sure if we'll ever find them." Edgar said.

"I know. I feel like our hands are tied, and I hate it. As long as he remains hidden, we will never be able to resolve this, nor will we be able to find those who are missing."

Chapter 19

Kurtis was both devastated and worried because of everything that happened. At that moment, it seemed like everything was falling apart. Just then, he heard a knock on the door. Veda answered it and noticed Steven Jr. and Simon standing there.

"May we come inside?" Simon asked.

"Of course." Veda said.

Simon and Steven Jr. stepped inside. They walked toward Kurtis who stopped what he was doing before he looked at both of them.

"Hello, Kurtis." Simon said.

"Hi." Kurtis said.

"We decided to stop by because we wanted to see how you were doing." Steven Jr. said.

"I'm doing terribly. Everything is falling apart. I don't know what to do." Kurtis said.

"We're both very sorry." Steven Jr. said.

"Don't you get it? All hope is lost. Afansi's family is gone, and Aston and Rose will never be able to have children. Both of their lives have been ruined by their father. I feel so sad for both of them, and I also feel powerless. I want to help them, but I don't know how. Also, because of what had happened, generations of their family will never exist, including the future warrior." Kurtis said.

"It just doesn't make sense. It has to be a mistake." Steven Jr. said.

"No, Junior. Endymion has won. We will never be set free from him." Kurtis said.

"Perhaps, not all is lost." Simon. said.

"How so?" Kurtis asked.

"There could be one other person who would be able to stop him." Steven Jr. said.

"Who?" Kurtis asked.

"You." Simon said.

"Me?" Kurtis said.

"Yes." Steven Jr. said.

"No, I can't." Kurtis said.

"Why not?" Steven Jr. asked.

"I'm no match for him. We've all seen what he's capable of and how powerful he is. The one person who may have been able to defeat him has been eliminated even before he had a chance to live. To be honest, I'm not even sure if he could've defeated him." Kurtis said.

"He could have, and he would've had he had the chance to. Unfortunately, that's been taken away from him." Steven Jr. said.

"What hope do we have now?" Kurtis asked.

"We have you." Simon said.

"I can't." Kurtis said.

"You were his forerunner. You're all the hope that we have left." Steven Jr. said.

"I'm not nearly as powerful as Endymion." Kurtis said.

"Perhaps not, but you have something that he doesn't." Simon said.

"What would that be?" Kurtis asked.

"You have us. Who does he have? We all stand behind you, Kurtis. With dad in no condition to lead, and with the chance of the future warrior existing now gone, we all look to you. You are our only hope, I, for one, stand by you, and I'm sure that many others do too." Steven Jr. said.

"I never wanted it to come to this, but I know that he must be stopped. I can't let him hurt anyone else."

Chapter 20

One night, while everyone was asleep, Endymion showed up at Kurtis' house. He made sure nearly everyone was asleep. Then he glanced around before he made his way over to Aston's room. When he entered the room, he stopped for a moment as he looked at his son, who was sound asleep. Then, he made his way over to his son's bedside.

"My dear son, I've heard about your affliction. My heart cries for you. If only you'd know how much I still love you. I know that I've said and done some things that I shouldn't have, and if

I could take it back, I would. The thing is, I was only trying to protect you." Endymion said.

Tears filled his eyes as he continued to speak.

"I know that there are some who think that I did this to you, but you must believe me when I say that I would never do that to you. I want our family to grow. I want you to have children." Endymion said.

Tears ran down his face as he kept his eyes on his son, who was sound asleep.

"You've been crushed because of this. You've been hurting both physically and emotionally, but I can heal you. I can remove that which afflicts you. I can remove it and make it all better." Endymion said.

He then attempted to heal Aston. Suddenly, there was a purple glow. Endymion then sighed as he spoke.

"It is finished. I have removed it. You will have that which you desire the most." Endymion said.

A tear trickled down Aston's face, even as he remained asleep.

"I hope that you will find comfort, now, my son. Never forget that I love you." Endymion said.

He stood up and as he turned, he spotted Rose standing in the room.

"Who are you?" Rose asked.

Endymion didn't respond.

"Are you another brother of Aston's?" Rose asked.

"No, I'm not."

"Then, who are you?" Rose asked.

"I am his father." Endymion said.

Rose was suddenly frightened as she kept her eyes on him.

"Calm down. You don't need to be afraid. I mean no harm. I was only trying to help." Endymion said.

"What did you do?" Rose asked.

"That, I can't tell you. What I can tell you is that hope is not lost for you and Aston. Do not give up on the thing that the two of you desire the most. The time is now, daughter-in-law. Go to him, but you must promise me that you will tell no one that you saw me, not even Aston."

"Why?"

"I know that I'm not welcome here. I also know that I've been accused of things that happened, but I promise that I had nothing to do with any of those things. I came because regardless of what people may say, I love my sons and I heard about Aston's affliction. I wanted to help him. The affliction has been removed."

"Very well, I promise not to tell."

"Thank you." Endymion said.

He thought for a moment before he froze Rose in place. He looked into her eyes as he spoke.

"You will not mention that I was here. In the morning, whenever you wake up, you will think that my being here was just a dream. When I leave, Aston will awaken. The time is now for you to do what you need to do. Do not give up. May both of you sleep well afterward." Endymion said.

He then caused Rose to unfreeze. They looked at one another for a moment before Endymion smiled as he nodded, and then he disappeared and went back to his home.